Bettina Valentino

and the Picasso Club

Niki Daly

Bettina Valentino
and the Picasso Club

Farrar, Straus and Giroux
New York

Copyright © 2009 by Niki Daly
Distributed in Canada by Douglas & McIntyre Ltd.
Printed in May 2010 in the United States of America
by RR Donnelley Company, Bloomsburg, PA
Designed by Jaclyn Sinquett
First edition, 2009
3   5   7   9   10   8   6   4

www.fsgkidsbooks.com

Library of Congress Cataloging-in-Publication Data
Daly, Niki.
    Bettina Valentino and the Picasso Club / Niki Daly.— 1st ed.
        p.   cm.
    Summary: A controversial new teacher at Bayside Preparatory School introduces the
exciting world of art to aspiring artist Bettina Valentino and her fifth-grade classmates,
encouraging them to see everyday life in a different way.
    ISBN: 978-0-374-30753-0
    [1. Art—Fiction.   2. Teachers—Fiction.   3. Preparatory schools—Fiction.   4. Schools—
Fiction.]   I. Title.

PZ7.D1715Bg 2009
[Fic]—dc 22

                                                                            2008003827

*Our heads are round to allow
our thoughts to change direction.*

—Francis Picabia

Contents

Bettina Valentino

and the Picasso Club

All About Bettina

Helloooo!

Yes, you! You, holding this book!

Are you reading me? Cool! We're connected!

Okay, this is all about me . . . *moi!*

Bettina Valentino!

And right now I'm refusing to open my eyes to face the beginning of a new semester. We've just had our winter break and spring is in the air. Spring's great because it means that summer's on its way. And I love, love, love summer! Especially when I open my bedroom window and see the bright sun sparkling on a turquoise sea. It makes me want to dive right out the window and straight into our dreamy bay. Simply gorgeous!

But at this very moment, I'm clutching my polka-dotted pillow and hanging on for dear life. You'd think I was holding on to the last life buoy off the *Titanic*, which in case you don't know was a huge ship that went down the plughole. But that was a thousand years ago, and this is now!

Like, NOW!

"Betteeena Valenteeeno! Time to get up, dear!"

That's my father calling.

"*Rubber duck!*" I groan. "Does he *have* to stretch my name out like an elastic band?"

PAUSE!

About school: It's not that I hate school. I simply find it a drag on Mondays. That's because art's on Mondays, and even though I ADORE art I definitely do not adore Miss Pyle, the art teacher.

Miss Pyle does things like brush inspection! At the end of every class, after we've cleaned up, she examines each of our brushes.

"Bettina Valentino!" Miss Pyle will say when she looks at mine. "Would you lick this brush?"

"Noooo!" I answer. Who on earth would lick a grubby old paintbrush?

"Well then, go and rinse it once more!"

Also, Miss Pyle's a big fan of repeat patterns. She says that repeat patterns MUST be done neatly, using warm AND cool colors.

Helloooo?

I'm the kind of artist who doesn't keep in-side the lines. I like art that jumps off the wall and hits you in the eye like a wound-up ninja. Art that's wild, expressive, and never, ever bor-ing. Get it? Besides, black and white are my fa-vorite colors. Miss Pyle says that black and white are not colors at all. She says they are the absence of color.

"Bettina Valentino," Miss Pyle will say, "may I suggest that you broaden your palette. Pastels are rather pleasant on the eye. Think pink, Bettina!"

Pink shtinks! That's what I think.

It's 7:30 and I've abandoned the polka-dotted life buoy. I've showered, dressed, had a bowl of cereal, and brushed my teeth.

Out in the driveway, Daddles has got old Roly Poly all revved up and ready to go.

Daddles is my dad, and Roly Poly is his 1962 Rolls-Royce Sil-ver Cloud II Convertible. He says it's a collector's item. I say it's a bad joke on wheels! Any minute now, it's going to choke to

death. Well, that's what it sounds like when Daddles tries to get it going in the morning.

As I head out the door, Mumsie says goodbye from the kitchen table. *"Au revoir, mon petit bonbon,"* she calls. She's a fashion designer and is always practicing her French, in case she ever gets to go to Paris to do a show.

Once we are on our way, Daddles takes a break from watching the road to question my personal appearance. "Have you combed your hair, dear?"

"Yesss!"

Freaking fish fingers! Has he forgotten that I was BORN with this fabulous hairstyle? I've actually got a photograph to prove it!

As we drive, Daddles says things like, "How're things, fairy wings?" and "Out of the way, Doris Day!" He makes up these silly rhymes on the spot. He thinks he's rapping. What a joke!

You have NO IDEA how embarrassing it is! Especially when he's doing it at a stoplight with the top down.

This morning, as payback, I'm thinking about slamming the door clean off old Roly Poly when we get to school.

But I don't do that. I'm nice. So I smooch the air and head for the school gates.

"See, you soon, potato moon!" he hollers.

• • •

I attend Bayside Preparatory School, otherwise known as
Blanche de Blaine's Academy for Slobs, Noodleheads, Nutters,
and the Madly Talented, such as *moi*!

Mum went to Bayside. And it hasn't changed much. It's still a
tiny school right near the coast. The building's ancient and a bit
psycho. Like, the floorboards creak as you walk down passages,
and there's this creepy fern-lined quad in the middle of the

building that we're not allowed to run across. If we're caught we have to stand on one leg for a minute.

The headmistress is Miss Blanche de Blaine. Mumsie has known her for years. "Blanche de Blaine, my foot!" she hoots. "She used to be Bernice Krotch when she was at school with Aunt Pinky."

To the teachers and kids at Bayside Prep, Miss Blanche de Blaine is known as Miss B. And Miss B runs "a tight ship." Well, that's what she tells our parents.

"Children require opportunities and discipline. And we, the Bayside staff, are here to see they get exactly what they need. But I must warn you . . . I run a *very tight ship!*"

This isn't true. Miss B and her school are more like . . . shipwrecks. The school badly needs a new coat of paint, inside and out. And Miss B just needs a new coat. In the winter, she wears gigantic old sweaters and a ratty full-length fur-lined leather cape. In fall and spring, she wears peasant skirts with frilly, kind-of-see-through tops and embroidered vests.

Mumsie says the gypsy look was all the rage in the seventies, and she ought to know. Right now, her own designs are going through a sixties retro phase. I'm her favorite model.

Someday I might become a supermodel.

8

My best friend, Carmen-Daisy Kravitz, calls me an *artyfarty-fashionloony*.

Carmen-Daisy adores words. Especially ones she makes up and writes down in that little notebook of hers. I call it her Little Book of Secrets, because she won't let me read it!

She says it's *con-fi-den-tial*.

That's another thing Carmen-Daisy does—splits one long word into pieces. It's more expressive that way, she says. And she should know, because she's going to be a famous writer someday. Carmen-Daisy says she finds people *fas-ci-nat-ing*.

I call her Nosey-Posey. She's always asking questions and writing things in her notebook.

"What are you writing in that book now?" I ask her this morning when I find her in the hallway. She has her nose to the page and is scratching away with a pencil.

"I've been interviewing people to name their three pet peeves. What are yours, Bettina?"

"Assembly, assembly, assembly," I say.

Assembly at Bayside Prep is held in the gym first thing every Monday morning, at eight a.m. sharp. Miss B has another name for it. She calls it "our Monday morning chat." Of course, the only one who gets to chat is Miss B. And Miss B always chats for far too long. Meanwhile, we kids all have to sit on our behinds on the splintery wooden floor and keep still.

She begins today like she begins every assembly: she holds a long-nailed finger to her lips until we settle down and go dead silent. As usual, she's wearing too much makeup. Her lips are red and smudgy, as though she's been sucking blood.

"Good morning, boys and girls!"

"Good morning, Miss B," we murmur. There are about a hundred kids total at the school, and it sounds like most of us have not woken up yet.

"Boys and girls, as we come back from our holiday to start the final term of the year, I'm afraid I have a bit of sad news."

There are a few murmurs, but Miss B doesn't keep us in suspense for long.

"Miss Pyle, our beloved art teacher, will no longer be with us. She has taken a job at another school."

I can barely stop myself from leaping up and pedaling the air with joy. Instead, I look at Carmen-Daisy, and feel the corners of my smile touching my earlobes.

"For the interim," continues Miss B, "we've appointed a replacement. Please join me in welcoming Mr. Peppard, our temporary *artiste* in residence."

She flutters her sticky eyelashes at Mr. Peppard, who is sitting on the stage next to a bunch of teachers. He stands up and waves. We all wave back and sing out hellos.

He looks nice, with a happy face and red hair that's mowed as short as a golf green.

"Look at what he's wearing!" whispers Meenah, another friend of mine.

I'm trying to work it out. Over a long-sleeved T-shirt he's layered a short red vest with frilly edging that sticks out around his waist. His flared trousers end above his ankles. He looks like a Caribbean pirate.

"He's wearing a blouse!" says BB, a boy in my class.

Well, I don't care. I think he looks . . . *cooluscious*!

Taking a Line for a Walk

Later that day, when it's the fifth grade's turn for art, we get to meet the cool-looking pirate in person. As we march into the art room, the first thing we notice is that he's not wearing shoes.

"In-ter-est-ing!" Carmen-Daisy whispers in my ear.

Daddles would call him a "character."

Mumsie would say, "Too *très* divine!"

I walk past him to my usual seat and sneak a peek at his toes. Some people's toes are weird, but he's got nice-looking ones.

"Hi, everyone. My name's Andrew Peppard. But most kids call me Mr. Popart."

Meenah giggles.

Mr. Popart smiles.

I fall in love.

And Carmen-Daisy catches it all!

She slides her all-seeing eyes sideways and sneaks out her notebook to scribble a line or two.

I know Mr. Popart's telling us something important, because I see his lips are moving. But my brain has turned into a mushy marshmallow goo, and I can't understand a word he says.

Carmen-Daisy nudges me with her pencil and I snap out of it.

"Now, if you're wondering why I am barefooted, I can explain. You see, the earth has so much energy that . . ."

But I'm gone again. I'm walking down the aisle in a frothy

white dress toward my husband-to-be: Mr. Adorable Andrew Popart. I actually hear him say "I do!" and that brings me back to Bayside with a shock.

"I do love teaching art. And even if some of you choose not to become professional artists one day, I'd love you all to become art lovers."

He asks us our names and we go around the room and introduce ourselves. Then he asks us something else. "So, tell me, what is art?"

BB goes first: "Art's like . . . stuff that's arty. You know, cool stuff."

"Art's anything beautiful," whispers Leo. Leo writes poetry and only speaks in whispers.

"I think art is very, very important," says Carmen-Daisy. "Just as important as math, or social studies, or any of the other subjects we learn at school."

Mr. Popart agrees.

Most of the kids have something interesting to say about art. Then Maxine Rattle stops nibbling her stubby fingertips and mutters, "Art's something you do when you're bored."

"Ditto," adds Ditto Cheesman. His real name is Ashley Cheesman. But since he agrees with *everything* Maxine Rattle says, we call him Ditto Cheesman.

"Those are all interesting comments," says Mr. Popart. "Now tell me, who are your favorite artists?"

BB says he digs Keith Haring: "Because he turned graffiti into art . . . or was it art into graffiti?"

Leo loves somebody named Paul Klee because, he says, his paintings look like pictures from a dreamworld. I wish I could say things like Leo says them. But I'm more of a painter than a poet.

Mr. Popart knows all about Leo's artist. "Klee was a Swiss painter of the last century who was famous for having a very unique painting style. He spoke about 'taking a line for a walk.' Now, what do you think he meant?"

"That's stupid!" says Maxine. "You can't take a lion for a walk!"

"A *line*, not a *lion*, pea brain," says Mason. Maxine spins around, and shoots out a pointy tongue—pointy and sharp, because it never has *anything* good to say about *anything* or *anyone*.

"What Klee meant is that you can draw a line in any direction and shape on paper. It's like taking a walk with a friend and going wherever you want to go," says Mr. Popart.

He's got such a nice way of explaining things.

"My mom once took me to see a dead cow in a big aquarium," says Meenah. "It made me vomit in the ladies' bathroom."

Meenah vomits a lot. We once went to the movies and she vomited into her popcorn during a car chase.

Mr. Popart flips through a fat art book at his side. "Oh, you mean this!" He gives us all a look at the photo of a cow cut in half, floating in a glass tank. "This is one of Damien Hirst's preserved carcasses," explains Mr. Popart.

We all make vomiting noises, and Mr. Popart laughs.

"I know, art *can* sometimes be very disturbing," he says.

On the other side of the group, I watch Mason secretly finish off his second Hershey bar. Then he sucks clean a chocolatey finger and holds it up.

"Yes?" asks Mr. Popart. "What would you like to add?"

"I'd like to add something to the toilet," says Mason. He is famous for being revolting.

"Off you go," says Mr. Popart, waving him out. We all know what's coming and wait for it: as Mason gets to the door, he gives his bottom a wiggle and pops one.

"*Re-volt-ing!*" says Carmen-Daisy.

"Excuse me, I thought I was teaching 'art,' not 'fart'!" jokes Mr. Popart. We crack up.

"So back to art! What about you? Who's your favorite artist?" He's looking straight at *moi*. He's got such lovely blue-green eyes . . . sort of greeny-grayish-blue.

"I adore Picasso," I say. "His art's so . . . so . . ."

"Abstract?"

"Yes, and he draws like . . . like . . ."

"A master?"

"No. I was going to say like a child," I reply.

"Oh, yes, yes, Bettina! *Exactly!* Picasso said that himself—that when he was a child he learned to draw like a master. And when he became a master he learned to draw like a child. Isn't that something?"

He shows us some Picasso pictures from his book.

"Well, I think his work is very weird and untidy," says Maxine. She always sounds as though she has a cold or something.

"I do, too," says Ditto.

"So, what art do you like?" asks Mr. Popart.

He smiles and waits patiently as Maxine clears her throat. "Well, ahem! I know what I DON'T like. And I DON'T like Picasso!"

She zaps me with a spiteful look.

"And Picasso doesn't like you either!" grunts Mason, back from his bathroom break. His rumpled boxers are sticking out of his jeans.

"Sir, did you hear that?" squeaks Maxine.

"Well, one thing's for certain," says Mr. Popart, trying to calm her down. "I can see we're going to have a very lively time working together. And that's the main thing, because art should never . . . ever . . . be boring!"

I'm so happy to hear that, I stand up and make a power fist. "YESSSS!"

I turn around and catch Carmen-Daisy busy scribbling in her precious Little Book of Secrets.

Give me a break!

Rock Art Rules!

$\mathcal{N}$ext, Mr. Popart shows us pictures of ancient rock art.

"Hey, that's like graffiti," BB Brown says.

We look at a cave wall covered with pictures that sort of look like humans, animals, and something in between. There are also scratchy marks, weird shapes, handprints, and patterns. Spooky! But I love it. And I love Mr. Popart for showing it all to us.

He tells us how African Bushmen lived, hunted, and danced to make rain fall on dry desert sand. He says they made their own art tools from sticks and feathers. For paint, they used charcoal, white clay, and also iron ore mixed with fat and egg and even animal blood.

Mr. Popart says, "I really liked BB's comment. So let's discuss the connection between graffiti and rock art."

"They're both painted on walls," says BB.

"And they both use pictures that look like toilet signs," says Mason.

"Those sign-like images or symbols are called *pictographs*," explains Mr. Popart. "And they're great at communicating ideas and important information. Public places, like hospitals and airports, are filled with pictographs that tell people what they need to know—just as the Bushman used them as a language to share information and tell stories."

Now Mr. Popart has a surprise for us.

"Okay, what I'd like you to do for the rest of the lesson is make your own wall art in the hallway right outside this room. You can tell a story, send a message in symbols, or just make your own handprints and patterns to show that you were part of the action."

Then Maxine goes and nearly spoils it all.

"My mother says that graffiti brings down property values," she says.

"So does mine," says you-know-who.

"Not here!" says Mr. Popart. "As long as you have permission to draw on a wall, it's not a crime. And I say it's okay. Although you have to be quiet so as not to disturb other classes."

Everyone, except Maxine and Ditto, rushes to get paints and brushes. Pretty soon we're like a gang of hit-and-run graffiti artists, silently covering the corridor wall with amazing images.

"I do like your use of black and white, Bettina," says Mr. Popart.

I blush. I don't know what's happening to me. I feel as if I'm bursting out of my skin, like a fried sausage.

"Bettina Valentino," whispers Carmen-Daisy, "black and white *may* be your favorite colors. But you've just turned *bright pink*!"

"Oh, pink-shtink!" I say, and add a dab of black paint to her little know-it-all nose.

Trouble, Trouble, Trouble

The following day, on the way to visit the library at lunchtime, Carmen-Daisy and I march past Miss B's office, and guess who we see? Mr. Popart.

I grab Carmen-Daisy and pull her over to where we can hear what's going on. Since the door's open, I tell myself it's okay to listen.

Miss B's talking. Her voice sounds brittle, like it's about to break and shatter into splinters.

"Really, Mr. Peppard, personally, I have no objection to the mural. But I've had a call from one child's parents who are unhappy that you are encouraging impressionable young people to scribble on walls. The next thing we know, the whole school and then the neighborhood will be covered in graffiti. And you do know what that would do to property values, don't you?"

I gasp. "Maxine! What a creep!"

Carmen-Daisy covers my mouth.

"I'm really not responsible for educating parents, Miss B," Mr. Popart replies. "As long as I'm here, my job is to teach children art in the best way I know how to. And I do that by making my art lessons exciting."

I want to burst in and hug my hero.

"Well, I rather like primitive art myself," says Miss B. "However, these particular parents are discussing the possibility of making a sizable financial contribution toward the upkeep of our school, so we must consider their objections."

"Let's go!" Carmen-Daisy whispers, and drags me away on tiptoe, to avoid creaking floorboards giving us away.

I'm furious.

"Poor Mr. Popart! Imagine getting in trouble just for making art really fun for us!"

"When I told my parents we'd painted a mural in the hallway," says Carmen-Daisy, "they said it was high time that something was done to spruce up the school."

"I'll kill Maxine if she gets Mr. Popart into any more hot water," I tell Carmen-Daisy.

"Exactly *how* will you kill her?" she asks, slipping out her notebook and trying to write while she's walking.

"What are you doing?" I demand. Quickly, she shoves the Little Book of Secrets back into her pocket.

"You're writing about me again, aren't you?" I say, trying to snatch it. We burst into giggles and my arms go all floppy. Carmen-Daisy skips away, pretending to write down even more juicy bits of information.

"Hey, you two!" It's Mr. Popart. We turn and see him walking along in baggy yellow shorts and a T-shirt with the word SMART printed on it. The letters SM are printed in red, while the rest are in black.

AWESOME!

"If you're going my way, I could do with a couple of extra hands." He points to a few boxes and rolls of paper outside the main office.

We march over and Carmen-Daisy chirps, "We'd LOVE to help you, Mr. Popart, wouldn't we, Bettina?" I feel woozy and hold out my hands. Mr. Popart passes me a few rolls of colored paper. We walk on either side of him. I look at Carmen-Daisy. She looks at me. We're both as happy as kittens who've just dipped their whiskers in a dish of cream.

"I've got a great project for our lesson next week," says Mr. Popart. "Have you heard of the Dada movement?"

"No," says Carmen-Daisy. "That sounds like baby talk."

"Exactly!" says Mr. Popart. "Some people say it's from a French children's expression for 'rocking horse.' Others think it's just a made-up nonsense word."

"Is it dangerous?" I ask.

"*Very* dangerous," he replies with a grin.

"Do be careful, Mr. Popart," says Carmen-Daisy. She looks as if she's going to hold his hand. But she doesn't.

"Now, why would you say that?" asks Mr. Popart, stopping outside the art room.

"We . . . um . . . don't want you to get into any more trouble," I say quickly. I want to kick myself. We're not supposed to know that he's in any kind of trouble!

"Me? Get into trouble?" says Mr. Popart. "Don't be silly! Now, give me those delicious rolls of paper and go back to whatever you were up to."

We skip off. We're not supposed to skip in the hallways. But sometimes when I'm with Carmen-Daisy, I can't help it!

When we stop, I give her my freaked-out look. "So, Carmen? What do you think about this Dada thing?"

"Dada, dada, dada!" she says.

To me it sounds like, "Trouble, trouble, trouble."

Dada Day

It seems like six weeks instead of six days before our next art lesson. But it is worth the wait. The following Monday, when we march into the art room, Mr. Popart's standing on his head, making funny sounds:

> Da da ba da pa pa la pee
> La la voo doo shoo bi doo dee
> Da da shoo shoo la la loo
> Me me popart yoo yoo yoo.

"Bizarre!" says Meenah. She always says "bizarre" this and "bizarre" that.

BB goes, "Yo, that's cool!" He knows how to play the drums and picks up the rhythm in his fingers. *Snappety snap!*

Carmen-Daisy and I try to out-giggle each other as we twist our heads to see our crazy upside-down art teacher talking baby talk.

"Hey, Teach, you're loco!" says Mason, removing a sticky finger from his nose and twirling it at the side of his head to show just *how* loco he thinks Mr. Popart is.

Maxine drifts in and mutters, "Dumb!"

I want to kick her right back out the door. And I won't even mention how pathetic Ditto looks trailing behind her, nodding his big head off.

Just then, Mr. Popart bounces back onto his feet.

"Now, *that* was just to get us into the mood for today's class," he says, panting.

"What's that?" we want to know.

"Today, I'm going to tell you all about my favorite *ism*."

"Your *what*?"

"*I-S-M*," he spells out. "Take a seat and I'll tell you about it."

Mr. Popart leans against the teacher's table. On it is an old metal kettle and some bits of junk.

"An ism," he says, "is something that you believe in *and* practice. For instance, if some of you believed that peanut butter spread on crackers made great art, you might call that *Peanut-Butterism*. And those who believed it and practiced making this kind of art would be called *Peanut-Butterists*."

"Or just crackers!"

If that had come from anyone other than Maxine, I would have laughed. But it's the *way* she says things that makes them sound nasty, and the way she turns around to see if anyone's laughing at Mr. Popart. Well, no one is.

"It's so stupid!" she says, looking at Ditto for support.

"Yeah, stupid!" Ditto agrees.

"That makes you stupid, and her the *Stupidist*," says Mason. He sure knows how to get a laugh. He's got this lazy way of talking and he scratches himself all the time, like he's too big for his skin.

But Maxine goes all huffy. She'd nuke all of us if she got half the chance.

"No, I'm glad that Maxine made that comment," says Mr. Popart. "That's exactly the reaction most people had toward Dadaism when it first appeared."

"Dada *what*?" we holler.

"Dadaism was an art movement that started during the First World War."

"Nineteen fourteen to nineteen eighteen!" Leo calls out before I can. I remember the dates from our first-semester history project.

"It was a long time ago," says Mr. Popart. "But the idea of using art to shock people and poke fun at things is still a powerful idea for artists today. Dadaists had fun using art to make people question what they liked to think of as real and normal."

Then he holds up the kettle and says, "What's this?"

"A kettle!" some Einstein in the back row calls out before I can hold up my hand.

Boys!

"Yep, a normal old kettle," says Mr. Popart. He picks up a few scraps lying on the table. With three balls of putty he attaches each bit to the kettle and holds it up. We burst out laughing at the hilarious face with a spouty nose, nutty eyes, and a bottle-top mouth.

"Mr. Kettle!" shouts BB, rolling out of his seat.

When we stop our hysterics, Mr. Popart interviews Mr. Kettle:

"So, Mr. Kettle. What do *you* think of Dadaism?"

"I love Dada . . . and I love Mama!"

We crack up.

"And who wants to be an ordinary kettle when you can be an extraordinary work of art?" he asks.

Mr. Popart's voice is hilarious. He sounds just like Mr. Kettle—all high and tinny.

"I simply boil when people take me for granted!"

That joke makes some of us fall out of our seats and laugh until our tummies ache.

"Is everything all right in here?" Miss B is standing at the door, and we quiet down.

"All fine, all fine! Just a bit steamed up!" replies Mr. Kettle.

Miss B tries to smile but it makes her face go wonky. "Very cute, but perhaps you all can keep it down a bit," she says, and goes away.

Mr. Popart puts Mr. Kettle down. We settle back in our seats. I'm sore from all the laughing.

"That was a bit of Dada theater for you," says Mr. Popart. "But you get the idea that by changing the way we see everyday things, or turning everyday people on their heads, we can experience life in a *different* way."

31

Everyone gets it. Everyone except Maxine . . . and Ditto.

"I still think it's a stupid ism," she says.

"Or whatever," mutters Ditto.

For the rest of the lesson, Mr. Popart shows us Dada art. There's something that looks like a peeling billboard with strange words, letters, and numbers. One piece is just a bicycle wheel on top of a stool. Another is a gross-looking urinal from a boy's bathroom with the fancy title *Fountain*. Next Mr. Popart holds up a picture of a bull's head made from a bicycle saddle and handlebars. He says it's by Picasso.

"That's such fun!" I whisper to myself. But Mr. Popart hears me.

"I thought you'd like it, Bettina." He smiles.

Carmen-Daisy looks at me, but then our teacher gets her attention when he shows us how to make a Dada poem.

First, he cuts out a small piece of text from a newspaper: *Today's weather on the southern coast will be fair to mild with sunny spells.*

Next, he cuts apart all the words and collects the batch of paper pieces, dropping them into a small paper bag and shaking them up. Then he takes out the pieces, one at a time, and tapes them side by side in three rows on a piece of paper. Then he reads his beautiful new poem:

> Today's on southern spells
> Fair the weather be mild
> With sunny coast to will.

"That doesn't make *any* sense," complains Maxine when Mr. Popart finishes reading.

"But it *sounds* nice, Maxine," says Carmen-Daisy.

Then she does her BIG Carmen-Daisy sigh:

1. First she breathes out all the air in her lungs, and she stops breathing for a moment.
2. Then she rolls her eyes as if they're following a dizzy fly buzzing round and round.
3. Next she takes a deep breath like she's going to explode any minute . . .
4. And then she quietly sighs.

"It does sound nice, doesn't it?" says Mr. Popart. "And you know," he adds, "I can see pictures that go with those words. Try listening with your eyes closed."

I squinch my eyes shut. He repeats the Dada poem and I *can* see pictures! When I open my eyes to peek around the room, I

see that almost everyone is smiling and nodding. Except Maxine, whose eyes are wide open and glaring at me!

Ditto opens his eyes and seems about to describe what he saw, but his face goes blank when he sees Maxine's expression.

By the end of the lesson those two are the only ones who don't want to be Dadaists.

When Mr. Popart hands out our homework assignment, there's loads of excitement: we must make a piece of Dada art—a painting, a sculpture, a poster, ANYTHING!

"As long as it's exciting and makes us see everyday life in a different way," says Mr. Popart. "And you'll have a real audience, too."

He tells us that he'd like our class to invite our parents to an informal Dada art show on Friday, right after school!

As I leave, I give Mr. Popart one of my special smiles. But before I can make my eyelashes go flippy-flappy like a butterfly, Carmen-Daisy yanks me through the door.

"Bettina Valentino! Quit flirting with Mr. Popart!" she scolds.

Honestly!

"Oh, flirty-shmirty, da da da!" I giggle.

Ditto turns around and smiles at us—a funny smile that makes me think that he's not a one-hundred-percent creep. Maybe, he's like . . . ninety-nine percent.

"Oh, come on, you four-eyed jerk!" snaps Maxine.

She's so savage!

Poor Ditto, he almost jumps right out of his Bart Simpson socks.

Smart Art

Carmen-Daisy and I work every day after school on our Dada projects—one afternoon at Carmen-Daisy's, where her mom huffs and puffs away on her Dada-looking exercise machine, and the next at mine, where Mumsie rushes about the house with pins in her mouth and rolls of brightly colored fabric, and Daddles, who also works at home, keeps popping his head into my bedroom.

Today he appears right on schedule, as soon as we drop our book bags and settle down to work.

"What's up, buttercup? Do we really have to wait until Friday for a peek?"

"DAAAD!" I moan.

"Just asking," he says, and disappears.

Actually, things are not going terribly well. Carmen-Daisy's best Dada poem has been chewed up by my darling dog Max, who is a four-legged shredding machine! And me? I keep changing my mind. I try one idea after the other and can't stick with anything.

Today my first idea is to melt an old Barbie doll over a candle and call her "Barbiecue." But that seems dumb. Then I am inspired to frame a silly photo of Daddles from his high-school days in which he's mooning the camera. I put a smiley face sticker across his bottom and make a label for the frame that says, simply, DADA.

"What do you think, Car?"

Carmen-Daisy looks up from her latest attempt at making a Dada poem. "I think you have newspaper stuck to *your* behind."

There *is* newspaper stuck to the seat of my pants. I twist around to read a headline: TROPICAL STORM RIPS THROUGH CARIBBEAN.

"Oh, gosh!" I say. "What if I made a dress out of a big trash bag . . . and glued headlines all over it? I could call my outfit Shocking Fashions."

"You could also add some recycled stuff," suggests Carmen-Daisy, waving Max away.

"Hectic!"

"*Hectic—electric!*" rhymes Carmen-Daisy. Then she looks at me and frowns. "Now what can *I* do to make this poem more interesting?"

"Me again!" At the door Daddles is poking his nose back into our business. "Whoa! Where'd you get this from, dudess?" he asks, spotting his embarrassing old school photo lying on the floor.

"You should be ashamed of yourself!" I tell him, using my best Miss B voice.

"What do you mean, young lady?" He picks up the photo and starts peeling off Mr. Smiley. "This was my application for the 1988 Bayside High Best Buns Competition."

"DAAAAAAD!"

"Okay, okay! Just want to know if Carmen-Daisy's staying for supper."

Her face lights up like a Christmas tree. Carmen-Daisy likes her food. She's very serious about it! And she adores eating with us because Daddles is such a good cook. So she nods her specs right to the tip of her nose. I push them back for her.

"I'll just have to let my mom know," she tells Daddles.

"I hope you like *passato di pomodoro alla panna*!" he says, showing off, and then zips away.

Carmen-Daisy looks to me for a translation.

"Tomato soup," I explain. "It's really yummy."

"What?" asks Carmen-Daisy.

"*Passato di pomodoro alla panna.*"

"Oh, you mean tomato soup," she says. We start giggling and make up silly names for other foods.

"*Anchovie vomitori!*"

"*Toastaroni lickaloony!*"

"*French Freddy's fried froggyleggies!*"

We laugh ourselves silly until I get a brilliant idea for Carmen-Daisy.

"Why don't you enlarge all the words of your poem and cut them apart into letters and turn them into a mobile that never stops making new words?"

"Brilliobonanzafantaroony!" she squeals. "I'll call it my Mobile Dada Word Generator."

At the table we are so jazzed by our new project that we can't keep our ideas to ourselves. Mumsie and Daddles love them both.

"*Fabuleux!*" says Mumsie. "I might even steal your idea for my next show, *ma chère* Bettina!"

I give her my NO-WAY look!

"Joking!" she says. But you can never tell with Mumsie. She gets her fashion ideas from all over the place, including me and Daddles!

I see Carmen-Daisy looking famished, so I offer her seconds.

"Ooh, *drool-i-cious!*" she says, and passes her bowl to Daddles. It looks so clean that I wonder if she licked it while no one was looking.

In the cafeteria on Thursday, we discuss our ideas for the Dada project. The show is just one day away, and we are psyched.

Leo says he plans to turn his saliva into ART. *Eurgh!*

"I'm going to spit into paper cups and sell it," he explains. And he's *serious!*

"That's like so *bee-zarrre!*" groans Meenah.

"Throw up, Meenah! Throw up!" jokes Mason. "We can sell that, too!"

Meenah sticks her finger down her throat and leans over Mason.

"No way!" he shouts, trying to escape.

We all scramble out of Meenah's way as she pretends to throw up. It's really more funny than sick. But it's not Carmen-Daisy's kind of fun.

"Calm down, children!" she says.

We do. We *always* listen to Carmen-Daisy when she talks to us like a granny. I catch my breath and fix Meenah's ponytail ribbon, which has come loose in the tumble.

"What are you doing for your Dada assignment, Meenah?" I ask.

"It's a surprise," she says, not giving *anything* away with those big toffee-colored eyes of hers.

"I'm going to make a one-man Dada band out of junk," says BB. He says there's a scrap yard in his neighborhood, and he's already collected tons of stuff to choose from.

And then comes the shocker.

"I'm framing my dog's poo," says Mason, just like that!

"*WHAAAT?*" we yell.

"My granddad has this big old gold frame in his shed, and I'm going to use it to frame a lump of Benjy's dried-up dog-doo, which I'll spray-paint gold."

"And how's that supposed to be art?" asks Meenah, looking as though she might *really* throw up this time.

"Well, you know, it's like . . . you know, people are always saying that some art is original and other art's like . . . tired old doo-doo. Well, mine will be like . . . both of those things!"

"Your idea stinks!" says Carmen-Daisy, lifting her nose in the air.

"Exactly!" says Mason.

"*DIS-GUST-ING!*" croaks Carmen-Daisy, and stops feeding her face. "Anyone want my chicken nuggets?"

· · ·

After school, my best friend and I bump into Mr. Popart in the parking lot.

"How're the projects going?" he asks.

"We're finishing them today," I tell him.

"And are you going to shock me?" he asks with a wicked grin.

"Maybe," I say. Then I wonder. Will headlines about war, global warming, and the naughty pranks of movie stars really shock anyone? I mean, we're already so used to seeing them in newspapers and magazines all the time. But maybe turning something shocking into fashion will shock. Hope so!

"And what about you, Miss Kravitz?" he asks, turning to Carmen-Daisy.

"I'm doing something with words. Words that no one has EVER seen before," Carmen-Daisy says. Her hands swirl about as though she's polishing the air. She can be *sooooo* dramatic!

"Super! I can't wait for tomorrow's big event," says Mr. Popart. He swings a leg over his shocking-pink motor scooter. In spite of the color, I want to jump on behind and ride off into the sunset with him!

Instead, I spot Daddles in his gas-guzzling monstrosity and sigh.

Carmen-Daisy looks my way. "Want a lift, Car?" I say.

"No, thanks," she says. "My mom's picking me up. She's taking me to buy some wire for my mobile this afternoon."

"Then . . . last touch!" I pat her shoulder and dash off.

"Last look!" shouts Carmen-Daisy, spinning around to hide behind the statue of Old Boobs—otherwise known as Ernestine Bublé, founder of Bayside Prep.

"Last word!" I holler.

"Bye!" she yells back. Carmen-Daisy must *always* have the last word.

I see her peep out to check on me.

"See you!" I shriek, and quickly jump into Roly Poly and slam the door shut before she can open her mouth and score another point. Today I'm the winner of the silly goodbye game we've played since preschool.

Some Art Stinks

"Dada, wada, wow!" Mr. Popart exclaims after school the next day, as the fifth graders start to gather in his classroom. He's knocked out by our projects. There's everything from weird paintings to collages pasted thick with cut-up magazines and exciting bits of junk. Maxine comes in clutching something wrapped tightly in brown paper—probably too good for our eyes. Ditto's managed to put together a little robot out of a toilet-paper roll and bits of computer parts. I don't know if he knows it, but it actually looks a bit like him.

"No time to dawdle," says Mr. Popart. "You've only got an hour to put up your work, so we must hurry."

"Where's Meenah?" Carmen-Daisy asks, looking around.

"She said she's going to surprise us," I remind her.

"I . . . will . . . too," comes a zombie's voice out of a long cardboard box standing up against the classroom wall.

Carmen-Daisy opens the coffin-like container. Inside is Meenah! She's dressed in a sari and partly encircled by bubble wrap. There's a label around her neck: MEENAH COOVADIA. ASIAN AMERICAN. MANUFACTURED IN DETROIT.

"That's . . . where . . . I . . . was . . . born," drawls Meenah in a mechanical voice.

"This is so weird," says BB. "It makes me feel like we're all kind of products or something."

"It certainly does," says Mr. Popart. "Well done, Meenah!"

"You . . . are . . . most . . . welcome," she replies.

Mr. Popart and I help Carmen-Daisy with her Mobile Dada

Word Generator. We hang it from the ceiling, and immediately it starts to make new words.

HWOBY . . . QLOVNO.

"I love that!" says Mr. Popart. "It's so . . ."

"BUMFIZY," says Carmen-Daisy, seeing a new one starting to form.

"Can't think of a better word myself," says Mr. Popart with a laugh.

The art room is looking fantastic. Like a real art gallery. Leo places his paper cups on a small table at the door and starts to fill them with his "art."

Gross, but interesting!

"Are we all ready?" asks Mr. Popart finally. There are fifteen minutes to go before our parents arrive.

"Hey, Car, will you help me with my Dada dress?" I ask.

"Sure," she says, taking her eyes off her fascinating mobile for a second. Not only does it make new words, but it also looks great in the colors and shapes she's used for the letters.

We dash down to the girls' restroom and are almost flattened by Mason, who is charging up the corridor. Only when he's a few feet away from crashing into us do we realize what he's carrying—his doggie-doo art!

I scream, leaping out of the way.

"Three words, Mason!" yells Carmen-Daisy as he passes. *"DIS-GUST-ING!"*

In the restroom, Carmen-Daisy's careful not to damage my Dada dress. She takes it out of the big black suit bag as though it's a ball gown. Then she carefully slips it over my head as though she's dressing a model. I spin around and it rustles like a cheerleader's pom-pom.

"What do you think, Car?"

"SHOCKASHAKERCHICA-LICIOUS!"

Golly, she really doesn't need a Mobile Dada Word Generator to come up with good ones.

"What do you think Mr. Popart will say?" I ask.

"Let's go and find out!" she says, and we fly back to the art room.

As I clank into the art room, I hear Miss B welcoming parents in the reception area down the hallway.

"Right this way," she says, like a tour guide leading a group of kids around the White House. In the classroom we find Mason holding his granddad's gold picture frame, but looking quite miserable.

"It was stuck on just a minute ago!" he explains to Mr. Popart, pointing at a smudge on a grubby piece of cardboard.

Oh dear! He's lost Benjy's poop!

"Well, I think it's really an original idea, Mason," says Mr. Popart, "but maybe the smudge will make the same point. Let's hang it up as it is for now."

He takes the frame and hangs it near an open window. Right then, Miss B marches in with our parents.

I see Mumsie and Daddles and wave. I'm hoping my dad can act normal for once.

But there's really no need for me to worry, because suddenly Mrs. Rattle starts shaking her leg like a dog with fleas. There's a brown thingy, speckled with gold, dangling from the spike of her high-heel shoe.

"Hey, you found my art!" shouts Mason.

I want to collapse with laughter, but everyone else is frozen, waiting to see what will happen next. When Mrs. Rattle realizes what she's stepped in, she has a screaming fit.

"Get it off, Harold! Get . . . it . . . off!" she shrieks.

"Well, do stop shaking your leg for a minute, dear, and I'll see what I can do," says Mr. Rattle.

Pooey! A pong spreads through the art room. More windows are flung open, and we all start shaking with laughter.

"Okay, let's calm down," says Mr. Popart. "I think Mason's art has caused quite a sensation, but there're many more wonderful pieces for you to see."

"I think I've seen quite enough!" says Mrs. Rattle. "Harold! Give me back my shoe!"

"Yes, dear. But we do want to see what Maxine has done, don't we?"

Mrs. Rattle shoves her foot back in her shoe and pulls her clothes straight. Thank goodness that's over! At last, our parents can start looking at our art.

The parents circulate around the art room, buzzing with questions and compliments. Everyone thinks our assignments are amazing. Except Mrs. Rattle. She's still fuming.

"Relax, dear," her husband says. "I . . . I'll get you something to drink."

I can't believe my eyes! He goes over to the little table near the door and grabs one of Leo's cups.

"Drink this down, dear. It'll do you good," he says, handing her a paper cup. Carmen-Daisy and I watch as she glugs it down in one swig, then pulls a face.

"Well, *that's* not what I'd call a cocktail," she says.

Carmen-Daisy looks as though she's going to go into hysterics. I put her off with a quick shake of my head. *Jeepers!* If Mrs. Rattle ever finds out what she has just swallowed, there will be an even bigger disaster than the sinking of the *Titanic*.

Thank goodness for Mr. Rattle.

"Do come and look at Maxine's wonderful self-portrait," he suggests, leading his wife to their daughter's exhibit. In her picture, she looks as if she's been given an electric shock. She's used the hardest, sharpest pencil in the world and ripped the

Maxine
Rattle

Gr 5

paper in some places. It's almost like she's murdered herself. It's too awful to look at.

But Mr. Popart joins the Rattles and says, "I find Maxine very interesting. She certainly knows what she likes and does not like about art."

When he moves away, I hear Mrs. Rattle mutter, "What a ridiculous man!"

I want to push her right off her high heels. But suddenly Daddles appears.

"What a brilliant idea!" he says, turning me around to view the recycled objects and read the headlines.

"Bomb threat closes school. Unidentified body found in alley. AIDS crisis worsens in South Africa. Drought threatens southeastern farmers."

"Wow, such a chic dress made with such dreadful news," says Mumsie, coming through the crowd. "It's really a powerful piece, Bettina."

"Smart art by my apple tart!" says Daddles. Before I can disappear, he gives me a bear hug. But we break apart at the sound of a bloodcurdling scream.

"I DON'T BELIEVE IT!"

Oh no! Mrs. Rattle has discovered the sign on Leo's table of paper cups: GENUINE ARTIST'S SPIT, $2.

Desperately, Miss B pushes her way toward an exploding Mrs. Rattle. Mr. Popart, standing underneath Carmen-Daisy's mobile, covers his eyes. Above his head, a new word is forming:

And that's exactly how he must feel right now!

Poor Mr. Popart!

For the entire weekend I can't get Mr. Popart off my mind.
I'm sure the Rattles are going to force him to leave Bayside
because of the trouble at the Dada exhibition.

"I don't think they can do that," says Daddles.

I stare at my mixed-berry-and-cream croissant. We always
have them on Sunday mornings. But I can't eat mine.

"Eat up, darling, and stop worrying," says Mumsie, patting my
hand.

A sick feeling in my tummy tells me that something dreadful
is going to happen in the coming week. I comb swirling patterns
in the cream with my fork. What if, at assembly tomorrow, Mr.
Popart gets the boot? What if he's humiliated before the entire

school? I can't bear to think of it happening to such a wonderful teacher. He's so kind and says encouraging things about everyone—even that beastly Maxine.

"Know what?"

Mumsie and Daddles stop talking.

"Mr. Popart's the best teacher in the entire world . . . universe, even," I tell them.

"He certainly knows how to challenge and inspire his students," says Mumsie. "I've never seen you kids so excited about art before."

"I've never seen Mavis Rattle so excited before," says Daddles. It's a funny joke, but I'm too worried to laugh.

At assembly on Monday, Carmen-Daisy and I swap nervous looks as we all sing the school anthem. We're not standing together, because Maxine and Ditto have pushed between us at the last minute. Maxine looks puffed up. The minute we stop singing and sit down, I feel certain that something awful is about to happen.

"Girls and boys," Miss B begins. (One week she says "boys and girls," and the next "girls and boys"—she's good that way.) She clears her throat, sounding like a frog warming up for a long croak, then continues: "I've something important to share with you this morning. It's not often that I must make a decision that may have an enormous impact on the entire school."

Oh, no, here it comes.

I catch a glimpse of Maxine, her pointy chin up in the air. The corners of her mouth are pulled into a horrid smirk. My heart's beating like one of those little toys that can't stop jumping about once they've been wound up.

"I would not be doing my duty as headmistress of this prestigious establishment—our beloved Bayside—if I did not take the bull by the horns and act with alacrity when a situation comes our way," Miss B is saying.

Why does she have to use such big words?

And what does a bull have to do with Bayside?

The fidgeting begins. Even the staff look as though they want to push her off the stage and get on with things. Mr. Popart looks especially uncomfortable. Perhaps it's his clothes. His outfit is very boring today, very different from his usual bright, baggy outfits. In fact, he's looking like he's been forced to dress like a normal teacher.

Miss B has had a word with him. *I knew it!*

"So, let me get right to it," says Miss B, taking such a dramatic breath that she has to cough. "On behalf of Bayside, I've decided to accept an invitation to allow our fifth graders to participate in an art competition sponsored by the Smooth as Satin Paint Company. The first prize, which will go to the winning artist, is five hundred dollars and a generous supply of art materials. This is a wonderful opportunity to showcase the unique talents that are nurtured at Bayside."

So that's it? An art competition? My shoulders feel as though they've sprouted little wings. I want to fly up and sprinkle drops of sparkling happiness over Bayside.

I look sideways and see Maxine's mouth drop. She looks like a goldfish whose bowl has just crash-landed.

I can breathe again. Mr. Popart may look weird, but at least he's safe.

"Know what?" says Carmen-Daisy at lunchtime.

"No, tell me."

"Maxine hand-delivered a letter from her parents to Miss B this morning that says if Mr. Popart is not kicked out, they won't pay to get the school painted and Old Boobs cleaned up over the summer."

"How do you know?"

"Ditto told Mason. And Mason told Meenah. And Meenah told me."

"Ditto *told* Mason?"

"Yes. I think even he's starting to get sick of Maxine. And you know what else?"

"What?" I ask, amazed at how much Carmen-Daisy knows.

"Well, Meenah heard Miss B yelling at Mr. Popart on Friday after the exhibition."

My toes are curling up with curiosity.

"Yes, Miss B told him that if he wants to stay at Bayside next term, he has to clean up his act. So that's why he looks as though he's borrowed a suit from an old uncle and is wearing shoes. And *that* means he's not getting the energy he needs from the earth."

Wow, *that's* why Mr. Popart looked so sad at assembly! Like Superman forced to wear kryptonite sandals, he's being drained of his energy.

I peck at my least-favorite school meal—chili cheese dog. Across the cafeteria, Maxine's on her own, gnawing away at her food like an irritable hamster.

"Where's Ditto?" I ask.

Then we spot him sitting with a bunch of nerds from his computer group.

"See?" says Carmen-Daisy. "Even little toads get sick of their witches."

• • •

Art follows lunch, and I want to see how Mr. Popart's doing.

"Hurry up, Car!"

The scatty thing's got her head stuck in the sleeve of her art smock. I pull her into shape and we rush to art. Mr. Popart smiles when we greet him. But something's wrong. It's like his battery's gone flat.

"I've got brochures for all of those who wish to enter the art competition," he tells us. Even his voice sounds sad. "And I've collected a pile of art books and magazines to help inspire you. Bettina, will you please hand out the brochures? And, Carmen-Daisy and Maxine, will you please pass around the materials?"

Maxine walks over as if she owns the school. She grabs a book for herself and leaves Carmen-Daisy to hand out the rest.

"Remember when I explained the meaning of an ism?" says Mr. Popart.

We nod.

Maxine mutters, "Oh, not this again!"

"Maxine, how much did your parents pay for your lobotomy?" asks Mason.

"Mason! That's mean," says Mr. Popart. "I suggest you apologize."

"Sorrrrry," says Mason, but when the teacher looks away, he lifts his rear and zaps her under the table.

Mr. Popart continues: "Well, there are many isms which you

will find in the reference books. Some you will like. Others won't appeal. The pictures are simply to inspire you. Although I must say, considering last Friday's controversy, Dadaism might be one to avoid. Still, there are so many other movements to consider. Cubism is one I find fascinating."

"What kind of art is that, Mr. Popart?" I ask.

He opens a thick art book and flips to a portrait. The face looks like it's been assembled willy-nilly from a bunch of different jigsaw puzzles. It's a Picasso. I love his art so much that I can tell if something's been done by him even if I've never seen it before.

I can also tell that Mr. Popart is getting back some of his old oomph as he explains Cubism to us.

"Cubism is a way of painting that does not show what artists actually see, but rather what they think an object would look like if you saw all its sides at the same time. For instance, look at this painting by Picasso. See, no one has a face that looks like this. It's as though all the features—eyes, ears, nose, mouth—are taken apart and then put together in a different order. That's called 'abstracting.' Have any of you heard of 'abstract art'?"

We have. On our last field trip with Miss Pyle, we visited a modern art gallery.

Mr. Popart closes the book. "So, some of you may decide to work in an abstract way and paint something that you feel, or have thought about in a different way. Others may decide to paint something that looks real. Picasso painted in many different ways, and Cubism is just one of them. He never stopped challenging himself, or his viewer. That's why I think he's one of the greatest painters of all time."

"I bet Picasso wouldn't even come in third in an art competition," I hear Maxine whisper to Ditto.

I turn around to defend my hero but am amazed when Ditto contradicts her. "I don't know, Maxine," he says, loud enough for some of us to hear. "I actually think Picasso's art is pretty cool."

Others chime in to agree, including Mason and BB.

Maxine looks like she wants to bash poor Ditto's head in with her dopey Welcome to Worm World pencil case.

Instead, she just makes another witchy remark. "Oh, yeah? Well, why don't you all just go and start up your own little Picasso Club?"

What a great idea, I think.

The Picasso Club

The first meeting of the Picasso Club takes place a few days later at my house after school. Mason, Carmen-Daisy, BB, and I are getting together to work on our entries for the competition.

"I'll tell my dad that he's not allowed to come into the garage. I mean our studio," I tell them.

"Hey, your dad's cool," says Mason. "I like the way he raps."

"Have a Coke, bloke. Want a cookie, rookie?" BB's impersonation is very good, and he keeps it up until Carmen-Daisy decides it's time to get down to business. She advises us to "think big."

"Big art really gets more attention than itty-bitty art," she says, like she's some expert.

"Except for itty-bitty doggie-doo," jokes Mason.

Soon we get busy. I adore the smell of art materials. Especially the smell of poster paint being mixed in jelly jars by Carmen-Daisy. Car suggests that we use this session to think up lots of ideas and then choose the best ones to work on. BB is bent over his sketchbook, drawing like a fiend. Mason just sits staring at a white sheet of paper, as though a cool idea is going to jump out of its nothingness for him to grab. I spend a moment with my eyes closed. Sometimes ideas just come to me when I close my eyes. Yep! A painting is starting to form in my mind. The trouble is that when you try and put onto paper something that's in your head, it doesn't always look the same. Art's difficult. But as Mr. Popart taught us, there's only one way to make art, and . . . that's to DO IT! So I start making little marks on a piece of paper, and before long I begin seeing shapes and get a feeling that something exciting could suddenly happen. And it does!

"Hey, that looks like my granny's flowery panties blowing in the wind," jokes Car, leaning over me. I giggle and push her away.

After an hour or so, Daddles swoops into the studio with a tray of litchi juice and leftover sushi. I can't believe my ears when he starts his nonsense:

> Hey, you dudes of da Picasso Club,
> Big Daddy says it's time to pack it up.
> Too much art makes da brain go mooshy,
> So chill out and have some sushi.

I consider drawing a black hole on my paper and disappearing through it! But Car grabs hold of me and squeals with greedy delight, "Oooooo, I lurrv suuuusheeee!"

Honestly! Sometimes, I think she'd go "Oooooo!" if I offered her some of Max's dog pellets.

The rest are not all that keen on sushi, so they glug down their juice and shove off. That leaves Carmen-Daisy with a tray of sushi.

"Know what?" she says. I wish she'd eat, *then* talk. But she can do both.

"What?" I ask.

"I kind of like Mason. So, okay, he's *re-pul-sive*. But he's also very *a-mus-ing*."

We start talking about Mason and the other boys in class.

"And what about Ditto?" I ask. "He's a surprise. I hear he wants to do some sort of computer art for the competition."

"Maybe we should invite him to join the Picasso Club," says Carmen-Daisy.

"Maybe," I say. But I'm not really paying attention. I drive Carmen-Daisy nuts when I don't listen to her. She says it's like I'm at home but not answering the doorbell.

"Hey, zombie-girl, are you listening to me?" she prods.

I'm not. I'm trying to work on my idea for the competition. But she's making such a gooey-chewy sound that I can't think. Out of the corner of my eye, I see her take out her notebook and go *scribble, scribble, scribble*. Sometimes I feel like she can read my thoughts. So I stop thinking for a while. But that's TORTURE for me. So I lean over and say, "Let's see what you're writing."

"No way!" she says, snapping her book shut. Clutching it, she gives me a wicked smile with that little sushi-filled mouth of hers.

Brat!

I'm feeling so inspired by the competition, I can't think about anything else except painting, painting, painting. When I'm at home, I work on more ideas in the studio. At school, I daydream about what pictures I'm going to work on when I get home. One idea is to paint a Cubist portrait of Miss B. She's already kind of weirdly Cubist-looking. Or I could paint something wild like Picasso's *Guernica*. Only it will be in black and white, using positive and negative shapes. And then I could do a sort of graffiti thing with aerosol paints. Trouble is, I've got too many ideas but I'm not completely happy with any of them so far.

65

One thing I know for sure: my painting's going to be BIG. No, HUMUNGOUS. I'll have to stand on a ladder to reach the top. It's going to have a lot of *feeling*. Definitely, it's going to be abstract. VERY ABSTRACT! It's going to be—

"Bettina, read on."

Mr. Graham, our English teacher, interrupts me in mid-daydream. *Fuzzballs!* I've no idea where they've got to with *Little House on the Prairie.*

"Forfeit, forfeit!" the class chants.

That's what happens in Mr. Graham's class when we lose our place in group reading—we must pay a forfeit. Mr. Graham loves making up forfeits.

"Okay, Bettina," he says. "Let's hear you do 'This Little Piggy' in a baby voice."

I plonk down in front of the class and kick off a shoe. I'm wearing my zebra socks with little toe pockets. Everyone giggles when they see me wiggle them. In my best baby voice I recite:

Dis liddle piggie wenna markit,
Dis liddle piggie stay hom.
Dis liddle piggie had wos bef,
Dis liddle piggie had noooon.
And DIS liddle piggie wen weeee
    weeee weeee
All da way hom.

It's a hoot! Lots of laughs! And it wakes me up. But soon I'm back to daydreaming again.

In our next class with Mr. Popart, he looks happier. He's wearing his "normal" clothes—an evening suit jacket, checked golf shorts, and . . . he's painted his toenails! I know he's feeling like his old self again because he's back to whistling. Well, not really whistling. I think whistling is a bit cheesy. He does a sort of breathy humming. I think they are all classical tunes, 'cause he sometimes makes the sound of exploding drums and blasting trumpets. But all very privately. So you have to be near enough to hear the concert.

This week turns out to be special. Why? Because his lesson's all about POP ART!

Finally we get to hear about where Mr. Popart gets his name.

We learn that Pop Art is art that uses everyday objects from modern life. Like soup cans, advertisements, and all kinds of stuff we find around us—even comics, food, and kitchen things. Mr. Popart explains that this art movement was started by the Dadaists but became very cool during the 1960s.

He says that Andy Warhol is his favorite pop artist. He shows a photo of Warhol, whose hair sticks out like mine. Only his is a platinum-blond wig.

"Andy Warhol started his career as a commercial artist by drawing shoes," Mr. Popart tells us. "He decided that making art for art galleries was no different from making advertisements. He even called his studio the 'Factory.' He made art as though it was any other product being manufactured in a factory. You can say that Warhol and his art were very much part of popular culture, just like pop musicians and their music. In fact, he said that we *all* could look forward to at least fifteen minutes of fame in our lifetime."

Next Mr. Popart says it's time for us to get busy practicing for our fifteen minutes of fame by working on our contest projects.

For the rest of the period, we look through Mr. Popart's books and cut out pictures from magazines for our "ideas" folders. It's great when the whole class works together.

Although the Andy Warhol pictures are fun, I am still in my Cubist phase. I cut apart a few fashion photos from a glossy magazine, jumble them together, and make Cubist faces for my folder. Carmen-Daisy leans over me and whispers, "If anybody's going to win an art competition, it's you, Picassolini!" I giggle and shove her away. She smells of chili cheese dog and berry juice.

"Disgusting," we hear Maxine say. She looks as though she's just smelled something worse than Car's breath. We look for Mason, but he's in the front talking to Mr. Popart. As Maxine flips through the teacher's art book, her eyes are growing larger by the second. Soon they'll pop right out of her red face. When she sees us staring, she slams the book shut and turns to Ditto. I don't think he's listening to her, but she spits it out anyway: "I'm going to tell my parents! Mr. Popart's book is full of dirty pictures!"

I can't imagine what she's talking about, and it really doesn't matter, because right then the fire drill bell goes off.

Honestly, you'd think it was the bombing of Pearl Harbor. Miss Oxford told us all about it in history. The Japanese bombed us and then we bombed them. War is SO STUPID!! So is fire drill. Miss B instructs us to stay calm and collected and to walk briskly, not run. Flapdoodles! If I smelled smoke, I'd run my legs off. Except, of course, if Carmen-Daisy needed saving from the flames. I'd make sure she was safe first, and then run my legs off.

"Bettina Valentino!" I hear her wailing from behind as we trickle out the front door. "Help, help! Save me!" I turn around and see her pretending to be on fire. I notice that she's eating a chocolate bar while fighting off the imaginary flames.

Typical!

70

Bettina Paints Up a Storm

That afternoon, the Picasso Club meets, except for Leo.

"He's got chicken pops," Carmen-Daisy tells me.

I smile. She means "chicken pox." Poor Leo!

Instead, we are joined by Ditto, who arrives with a laptop. By standing up to Maxine's attack on Picasso, Ditto made himself a lifetime member.

I prop up a large white polystyrene board on Mumsie's old art-school easel. I like painting on polystyrene. The rough surface feels like a wall, and if you don't like what you've done, you can wash it all off under a tap. It's also nice and light to carry around. I use poster paint and fat bristle brushes. Carmen-Daisy uses little brushes that she smooths into a sharp point before she starts painting. I smile at her little ritual as she settles down to work at a trestle table. Mason decides to work on the floor with BB.

"I'll be okay on this chair," says Ditto, opening the laptop.

Just then, Daddles butts in.

"It's getting a little too quiet out here," he says, putting down a CD player and plugging it in. He presses the Play button and one of his stupid old favorites comes on.

"*Daaaaaaaaad!*" I groan. I can make it sound like a whale having a baby.

"Okay, okay! Just thought you'd like some inspiring background noise by my favorite rock group."

"No . . . we . . . DON'T!" I eject him and his CD, but the music idea is a good one. I dash to my room and find a hip-hop CD from my cousin Lily, who lives in Cape Town, South Africa. It's amazing stuff.

"Shake da bootie!" jokes BB in a fake South African accent, jumping up to wiggle his round bottom. "I dig it. I dig it!"

"Ditto," says Ditto.

We all shoot him a look.

"Cut that out!" says Mason, pointing his finger toward Ditto.

"Dittoditty?" says Ditto with a funny smile. He's quite cute when he smiles like that.

"That's better," I say.

"Discodittyhiphopodacious?" he suggests. He's getting cooler by the second.

"*Ex-cel-lent!*" says Carmen-Daisy. "Now, puhleeese, let's work."

By the end of the afternoon, we've done stacks. I've had fun being fierce with my paint. But it's not finished!

Carmen-Daisy has filled a small square with colors and patterns.

"I thought big is better," says Mason, unimpressed.

"This is my first square, see?" says Carmen-Daisy. "When I've done nineteen more, I'll tape them together and have a BIG picture."

"Hey, come and check this out!" says BB, leaning over Ditto.

We go over and look at the laptop screen. Ditto has taken his school photo and morphed it into a picture that looks like a famous painting I remember seeing before.

"I've combined it with this old Norwegian guy's painting called *The Scream*," says Ditto. His face really looks like he's screaming. Maybe he's thinking about mean Maxine.

BB's done a composition of handprints and graffiti-like marks covering a sheet of black paper. Great!

And Mason?

Whoa! Mason has carefully turned his white sheet of paper . . . black. But it's pretty amazing, because he's used a black ballpoint to cover the entire white background. Mind-bending!

"It's like . . . you look at it . . . and make your own picture. Get it?" he explains, spreading his hands over his picture of scribbled *nothingness*.

"I get it," says Carmen-Daisy.

"Ditto— Er . . . seriously cool," says Ditto, correcting himself.

When it's time to go home, Mason says, "Coming, Car?" I smile and flutter my eyelashes teasingly at Carmen-Daisy. Kissy kissy!

"Hey, Mason! Wait for me!" Carmen-Daisy calls. I watch her run after him. Just before she reaches the gate, she turns around and sticks out her tongue.

"Saw that!" I yell.

"No, you didn't!"

"Yes, I did!"

"Heard that!"

"No, you didn't!"

We're mental!

• • •

After they've left, I feel hungry. *Famished!* Making art's hard work. Daddles is in the kitchen, preparing dinner in a wok.

"I'm hungry," I announce. I open the cupboard and reach for my favorite snack—Froot Loops!

"Don't spoil dinner," says Daddles, making a grab for the Froot Loops.

"But I'm staaaarving."

"People in Africa starve. People in this country get the nibbles," he says.

Give me a break!

Just then Mumsie comes in.

"*Nouvelles terribles!* It sounds as though Mr. Popart's job is on the line," she says. I loosen my grip on the Froot Loops and listen. "I've just gotten an e-mail from the school. Miss B's telling all the parents that the Rattles are accusing Mr. Popart of showing dirty pictures of naked men and women to Maxine in class today."

"That's not true!" I say. It just can't be true. I burst into tears.

"Take it easy, sweetie," says Daddles, letting go of the cereal.

"I'm sure you're right," says Mumsie, "but he's been suspended. Apparently there's a parent-teacher meeting tomorrow night to discuss it."

I'm so upset that I have to go to bed. I don't even take the Fruit Loops with me.

It's true. The following day Mr. Popart's not at school.

My mind's a mess. In math I divide instead of multiply the number of eggs produced by a hundred red hens and one black rooster. It's a trick question. But before I can sort out the problem, the batteries in my calculator are as zonked as the poor black rooster. History's no better. When Miss Oxford asks me what's the Seventh Amendment, I answer, "It's one of the rules on the stone that Moses brought down from the mountain after meeting God in a burning bush."

The roll of her eyes tells me that I'm an idiot.

The sniggering sounds from Maxine are too painful to bear. I feel tears welling up.

Worse still, my drawing of a volcano for geography looks like a badly fried egg. When Mrs. McDermott asks why I've handed in such an untidy effort, I finally break into tears. I want to tell her that I can't stand how beastly Mr. Popart's being treated. But when I try to talk, I let out a wail as alarming as the fire-drill siren.

Miss B's called.

"Bettina, dear," she says to me out in the hallway. "Do pull yourself together."

Now what does THAT mean? Must
I pull my legs and arms together
and go into a KNOT? Adults can
say such stupid things! I
want to give her loopy
earrings a good pull until
her eyes light up! But
I bury my head in my
hands and sob.

"I'll call your parents,"
says Miss B. "Maybe you just need
to go home and rest. For now, why don't you
come with me and lie down on my couch?"

I've snotted up my sleeves and feel miserable.

"It's going to be all right," says Carmen-Daisy, who has
packed up my bag and brought me my things. Then I follow
Miss B down the hallway.

Mumsie and Daddles are very sympathetic. They both come
to pick me up.

"How about some nice crème vichyssoise, then into bed with
a nice book?" Daddles suggests when we get home.

I don't want crème vichyssoise. And I don't want bed. I feel
all mixed up thinking about Mr. Popart without a job and being
accused of such ugly things. My head's spinning, like a washing
machine stuffed with tangled-up socks.

I slip on one of Daddles's old shirts that I use for painting and
go to the garage. Roly Poly's there, but Daddles has left a space
for me to work on my art. I look at the first bold brushstrokes

that I made yesterday. My painting feels like a friend waiting to talk to me. I can say whatever I want to. I don't even have to open my mouth. I'm sure that's how Picasso felt when he painted.

And now I feel like I want to paint up a storm!

By lunchtime, Daddles pops in with a glass of Perrier and a bagel sandwich. He always serves me Perrier in a little gold-rimmed glass he bought in Venice. He says it improves the taste. He puts down the tray and comes to me. He puts his hand gently on my head and just looks and looks, and then says, "It's . . . it's . . . a wonderful painting, Bettina. What's it called?"

"I don't have a name for it yet." I tell him. "But it's for Mr. Popart."

"I'm sure he'll feel very honored," says Daddles. "I hope to see him this evening at the meeting."

"Please stick up for him, Daddles," I say. "Everyone's against him. And I know he's not horrible."

"We'll see what he has to say," says Daddles. "Now drink that down. I'm sure you're parched. And try to eat something."

I can't touch my sandwich, but I drink my Perrier and look at my painting. It's bold and abstract. You can see things in it if you want to. If you don't, you can just feel them. I look at my hands. They'll never be clean again! But that's okay. I once saw a photo of Picasso, and his hands looked like he'd been playing in mud.

At six, my babysitter, Connie, arrives. She's looking super in her short bolero, kilt, and tiger-lily tights. I study her boots while she chats to Daddles about our pizza order. This evening, we're sharing a jumbo Hawaiian. A pizza, not a person. I'm famished.

"Ask them to hold the banana," he says. "It makes it too mushy."

"I *lurrv* mushy banana," says Connie.

"So do I," I say. I'm a bit like Ditto when I'm with Connie. I agree with *everything* she says.

"We ought to be back by nine," says Mumsie. "Perhaps you'll be in your pj's by then, Bettina."

I will. But I'll be wide awake and dying for the news.

It's great being with Connie. I can talk to her about anything. When she hears about the lousy time I've had at school, she says I need some TLC. That means "tender loving care." So we stuff ourselves silly with mushy pizza and watch some dumb reality show. Contestants have to do all kinds of crazy things, like speeding down steep hills in shopping carts with only a golf club as a brake. When the program ends, I show Connie my collection of precious jewels. After that, it's a makeup session. I make Connie up to look really wicked.

"We'd better clean up and get you into your pj's before your folks get back," says Connie, steering me by the shoulders to the bathroom. By the time my parents return, my teeth are brushed and I'm ready for bed.

When Mumsie and Daddles see Connie with all her makeup, they laugh hysterically. Grownups are like that, aren't they?

Always laughing their heads off over this, that, and *whatever*.

"See you, Bettina!" Connie calls after chatting to Mumsie downstairs.

Then I hear my parents' footsteps coming up to my room.

"Oh, please let everything be okay," I whisper. I clutch Amelia, my gingham piggy. Amelia's lived on my bed since I was four.

"Hi, sweetie."

"Can Mr. Popart stay at school?" I ask Daddles.

"Well, it seems that he might have to go," says Daddles.

"Not that he's done anything wrong," adds Mumsie. "That was utter nonsense about Mr. Popart showing 'dirty pictures' to Maxine. They turned out to be a series of nude drawings by Matisse. Can you believe it? Your nana has a framed print of one of them in her lounge, for heaven's sake!"

"So why must he go?"

"Because the Rattles have threatened to withdraw a lot of funding from the school. And without it, Miss B feels that the school's going to fall apart."

"Miss B was quite decent about it," says Daddles. "When she saw the art book that Maxine made such a fuss over, she took Mr. Popart's side, as did all the other parents. But the Rattles stormed out of the meeting, saying they would be reporting Mr.

Popart to the police for being a degenerate. Poor Miss B just couldn't handle that. She said Bayside can't afford the scandal. Then Mr. Popart stood up and gave a little speech. He was *très* wonderful. He said that even though he was innocent of the charges brought against him by the Rattles, he would not fight for his job if it meant harming the school."

"Mr. Popart's not a *degenerate!*" I say. I'm not too sure what that means. But whatever it means, I KNOW that Mr. Popart's not one. Carmen-Daisy told me that he actually has a sick old mother he's looking after. So, you see, he's an absolute darling!

Fat tears plop out as I think about how sad it is to have a dear old mother who's dying.

"Oh, sweetie," says Mumsie, and wraps me in her arms. This makes me bawl even harder. Before I know it, Daddles is wrapping Mumsie *and* me up in his arms.

Mumsie whispers, "There, there!"

We stay like this for a while until I start feeling really hot.

"Thanks, Daddles," I whisper.

"My pleasure, treasure!"

Whew! I'm glad when they leave me to close my eyes and listen to the sea outside my window.

Soon, sleep washes right over me.

Ditto's Dead

The days that follow are as depressing as a soap opera, with no happy ending in sight. Mr. Popart's absence really hurts. You know how when the sun goes behind a gray cloud and time seems to stand still? Well, that's how it feels.

Art has been canceled. In its place we do drama. Flaring nose holes! If there's one thing I am not in the mood for, it's Miss B's drama instruction. To make matters worse, Maxine is a real ham. I can't bear listening to her enunciate her words as though she has marbles rolling about in her cheeks. Even when she's being a tree, she overacts. I've actually thought of murdering her. But, to be honest, I can't even fight the ants that fall into our bath. So I pretend she doesn't exist and stare out the windows of my classroom, waiting for the sun to come out.

The evening before our deadline, I complete my painting. The thick black slashes of paint look like my hair after it's been whipped up by a really wild wind. I have no idea if it's good or bad. If Mr. Popart were around, I could ask him. But he's not.

That night I have a horrid dream. I'm caught up in a spiky repeat pattern and can't get untangled. When I call for help, a creepy grinning face appears. First it's very Cubist, and then suddenly it turns into Maxine Rattle.

When I wake up, I'm tangled in my sheets and the shutters are clattering like castanets. The wind's wild and it looks as though a storm is coming over the bay.

Blast! I have to get my painting to school today.

Daddles helps me wrestle it into the back of Roly Poly. I've used such a lot of paint that some of it is still not quite dry. On the way to school, we drive over leaves and twigs scattered about. The sea is shivering in the bay. Yesterday it was blue, blue, blue. Today it looks like dirty dishwater.

De-press-ing!

That's how I feel. Depressed! With no Mr. Popart around, who's going to appreciate our entries? Miss B looks arty, but when it comes to judging art, she likes *everything*. And if you like everything, then you can't know what's really good, or what's really bad, can you? I mean, she even likes Maxine's psycho art. She said it was "very powerful and telling."

As we approach the school gates, it starts pouring. The wind's gone crazy. It's like we're going through a car wash.

"Don't worry, I've got a plastic tarp," says Daddles. When we park, he leans over and starts pulling the slippery sheet over my painting.

"Be careful! It's still wet in a few places!" I screech.

"Okay, okay," he says. "Shall I carry this for you?"

"Nooooo!"

Lordy, I don't need anyone to see my father in his see-through plastic raincoat, looking like Cling Wrap Man.

I slide out and pull the painting through the back door.

The wind's whipping against me and the plastic tarp is making it hard for me to grip. I find one edge and stretch to grip the other side. My arms want to snap. If Daddles makes up one of his silly rhymes, I'll let the wind blow me away, I swear!

"Take care, teddy bear!" he calls after me.

By clutching onto my flapping masterpiece, I've turned myself into a kite. Any second now, I expect to be lifted off my feet and blown across the bay. It's terrifying! When I'm halfway up the path, the wind tugs my painting right out of my hands. It tumbles across the lawn, picking up twigs and swirling junk that's been blown out of the recycling depot. I run after it, screaming. But the wind blows my screams away, and I end up making little mewing sounds. I bet I *look* like a drowned cat.

Then I hear Carmen-Daisy, coming from behind.

"Bettina!" she hollers.

I turn around, just in time to see her overtake me. I've never seen her move this fast. She reaches my painting when it stops for a while against Old Boobs. I follow her as she drags it indoors. It looks more messed up than I do. It's plastered with twigs, leaves, acorns, wrappers, bits of broken plastic spoons, and dirt. I'm wet all over, so no one notices that I am crying.

Carmen-Daisy starts pulling little bits off my painting.

"I'm sure we can make it nice and clean," she says. But she's making it worse.

"Leave it, Car," I whisper wetly.

Carmen-Daisy looks at me like Mumsie does when I am in the dumps.

"Miss B says we must go to the art room with our art, and then we have to fill in our entry forms. They must be handed in by lunchtime." I pick up my wrecked work and follow Carmen-Daisy to the art room. I wish Mr. Popart would suddenly appear and say, "Morning, Bettina!" But there's only Meenah, Mason, and Ditto around. I lean my painting against the wall. I don't want to look at it.

"Crikey! That's amazing!" says Mason. I throw forked lightning at him.

"No, I'm serious, Bettina. It's fantastic. How did you do it?"

He's not being funny. I look to see what he's talking about. It makes me examine my wrecked painting in a different way.

"It's like a new . . . ism," says Ditto.

BB joins us and starts raving as well. "Whoa! That's what I was trying to do. Make a grungy picture with footprints and stuff. But this is serious grunge."

"Grunge . . . ism," says Carmen-Daisy.

"What's that?" sneers Maxine, coming in with her work. She holds it as if it were Miss America's tiara.

"At least it's art," says Mason. "Yours looks like it's been done by a brain-dead lab rat!"

"Now, now, now! Let's not be negative about anyone's efforts," says Miss B, sweeping in. "Ultimately, it's the judge's choice," she reminds us. Then she stands back, looks at my painting over her fancy specs, and says, "Mmmm, very rustic." I make a note to look that word up. I'm not sure if it's a nice thing to say about anyone's work. But maybe it is.

"Now leave your masterpieces here and go to your home-room. They'll be collected and packed up at lunchtime. Then we must all cross our fingers and wait!"

Maxine moves her painting in the direction of Miss B and does a little LOOK-MY-WAY cough.

"Very controlled work, Maxine," says Miss B. "You never cease to amaze me."

• • •

Tuesday's lunch is always tacos—*another* of Carmen-Daisy's favorites.

"Hurry up with your taco."

I give her a nudge. She nibbles around the edges, filling up her cheeks like a hamster, and then chews. If I didn't adore her so much, I'd find her *re-volt-ing!*

"I'm hurrying!" she says, licking her plump fingers. "Now I'm finished!" she declares, and then does a refined burp behind her napkin.

We've got to dash. First to get our music sheets for choir practice. Then to hand in our entry forms, which we finished filling in at lunch. I've decided to call my painting *The Storm.* That's how I feel inside, and that's how the weather is outside.

Leaves, ferns, branches, and abandoned worksheets swirl around the quad. The wind has died down a little but we hold on to each other as we cross to the art room.

When I get there I'm shocked by what I see.

My painting—my painting that I've spent hours and hours on— has two holes in it.

"Someone's kicked in your painting!" says Carmen-Daisy.

I'm ready for combat, but there's nobody else in the room. Just then Miss B arrives, and Car tells her what has happened.

"Really?" she says. "How barbaric."

But Miss B also says that nothing can be done about it. I have to submit it as is. All the entries are being collected in an hour's time. I see my chances of even getting an honorable mention go down the drain.

Carmen-Daisy and I hand in our forms. Then we head for the music room.

But I can't concentrate on scales and *tra la la*'s. I keep seeing the two ugly gaping holes in my painting. Twice, I hit my tambourine too late. Each time, it makes Mrs. Perkins flinch as though someone's stood on her toe. After music is science. And if I don't start concentrating, I'll blow up the science room.

On our way to our lockers, Carmen-Daisy tries to cheer me up.

"Even famous paintings have been attacked by crazy people," she tells me.

"Name one," I ask.

"The *Moaning Lisa*," she says.

"You mean the *Mona Lisa*. By Leonardo da Vinci."

"Whatever. Two holes in a painting doesn't mean that it's not still a work of art."

This is supposed to make me feel better about entering a vandalized painting covered in junk. But it doesn't. I should have thrown it away. Plus, I think I know who's responsible. I wish I could talk to Mr. Popart about it. But I don't even know where he lives. I imagine him in a little attic room with his poor sick mother coughing and close to dying. *Oh, Mr. Popart!*

For a few seconds we walk without talking. A record for us! As we turn into the corridor leading to our lockers, we see Maxine and Ditto. They look as though they are arguing. Maxine's shrieking. For every word she spits out, she pokes Ditto in the chest.

"If you say just ONE word about it, I'll whack you!"

Her voice grates like fingernails across a blackboard. Ditto pulls away and turns toward us.

"I'm warning you, you goggle-eyed twerp!" Maxine shouts at his back.

As cool as a dude in a cool-dude movie, and without even turning, Ditto shouts back, "OH, SHUT UP, YOU MEAN-MOUTHED, PINHEADED LOSER!"

She looks as though she's been hit in the face with Mason Worple's stinky underpants.

Ditto holds his head high and throws up a power fist. *"Ditto's dead! Long live Ashley!"* he yells over his shoulder.

He comes to us and says, "Bettina, I've got something to tell you."

I already know what it is.

Within minutes, Ash and I are in Miss B's study, telling her what happened. Then Maxine is summoned.

"Now, young lady," Miss B says sternly to Maxine, "Ashley tells me that you damaged Bettina's painting."

"I did not!" Maxine screeches. "Her painting was messed up when she came to school."

"It didn't have two holes in it," I say.

"Maxine really did tell me she kicked in Bettina's painting, Miss B," says Ash. "She was bragging about it. She said it needed a few kicks to really finish it off."

"Did not," snaps Maxine. If looks were daggers, poor Ash would be in pieces.

But he stands up to her and says, "If I'm lying, then what are those paint marks on your shoes?"

We look down and see the telltale paint marks on Maxine's pink sneakers.

"He's a liar, Miss B," she hisses. "My mother says that people who have no earlobes are liars. And look, his ears go right into his neck!"

"I'll be having a word with your mother myself, so let's not hear about what your mother thinks. I think your behavior is absolutely unacceptable in a reputable school such as Bayside."

I've never seen Miss B looking so cross.

"I suggest you apologize to Bettina for your criminal actions and apologize to Ashley for your insulting remarks."

"But I didn't do it," Maxine sneers. "Just wait until my parents hear about this."

"They will hear about it sooner than you think. I'm going to ask them to come see me immediately. Maxine, you wait outside my office. Bettina and Ashley, you may return to class."

As we leave, Miss B says, "Ashley, I commend you on your willingness to come forward and report this incident. Revealing a crime is always noble."

I know that word. Knights are noble. Oh, noble Sir Ashley!

The Prize

"Know what?" whispers Carmen-Daisy in the library.

I'm all ears. I stretch my neck so that I can also read what she's written in her little book, which is starting to look quite grubby.

"The Rattles don't believe that their darling Maxine could do such a thing. They say they plan to sue Miss B for making unjust accusations."

"Shhhh over there!" says Miss Nightingale, our pretty librarian.

I squeeze up to Carmen-Daisy and whisper even more quietly. "How do you know all of this?"

"The Rattles are taking Maxine out of Bayside, and they have refused to give any of the money they promised Miss B to paint the school and make Old Boobs look new again. In fact, Maxine's gone for an interview today at that snobby Pankhurst School for Girls." She closes the book, makes googly eyes at me, and says, "I keep my ears and eyes open."

I could pull her nose! What a little snoopy-poop! But, I suppose, if Carmen-Daisy's going to be a famous writer one day, she's simply got to snoop around for stuff to write about.

At break, I have a brilliant idea: the Picasso Club will hold an exhibition to raise money for the school to replace the funds withheld by Maxine's parents. Everyone agrees to put in some extra studio time and produce stacks of art.

Ash, BB, Mason, Car, and *moi* are discussing the kind of art that will really sell when Meenah comes running toward us. She's all sweaty and breathless . . . with something important to tell us.

"I've just seen Mr. Popart. He's back in the art room," she gasps.

"*What?*"

She tells us that Miss Nightingale got a petition together and persuaded Miss B to ask Mr. Popart to return.

"I think Miss Nightingale fancies him," says Meenah.

I feel a jab of jealousy. I jump up. I want to see him for myself! The others follow.

It's true!

We find him working in the art room as if he's never left. When he sees us he holds out his arms, and before I know what I'm doing, I charge right into them, almost knocking him over.

"Hi, my favorite artists," he says as we crowd around him. When he hears about our plans for an exhibition, he says he'll help us in any way he can. *Superdoops!*

We ask him to attend a few workshops and give us some art tips. Then Carmen-Daisy tells him the sad story of my painting.

When he hears that I still entered it after all that happened to the poor thing, he says, "I think that's really adventurous, Bettina. Lots of artists would have pulled out of a competition. But it shows a belief in your work."

"It didn't look like mine in the end," I reply.

"But you *allowed* it go as it was—changed by accident. There's something special about art that includes accidents. Jackson Pollock spent his entire life allowing accidents to happen on his canvas. Look!"

He flips through a book and shows me a painting by Jackson Pollock. It's amazing. I don't like Pollock as much as Picasso. But his blobby, squiggly painting reminds me of what the storm did to mine.

Ash says, "Yours is better!"

I blush because Mr. Popart's looking sweetly at me.

"I think you're going to make a very fine artist one day," he tells me.

Aaaaaah! Mr. Popart always knows the right thing to say. That's what makes him such a great teacher. He teaches us to believe in ourselves.

An *absolutely* divine week goes by. And then Miss B tells us that she's received a letter from the competition sponsors. But, she wants to share the news before the whole school. I think she's getting carried away. I mean, this is not World Hip-Hip-Hooray Day!

Still, it's exciting. And the next day the hall's packed.

When everyone settles down, the staff comes onto the stage. Then Miss B makes her grand entrance. She does all the things she teaches us in drama. She glides. She arrives. She poses. She *projects*! She opens the envelope with trembling hands and says she's going to announce the winners in reverse order.

"Third prize goes to Abigail Mulholland of Pankhurst School for Girls."

Carmen-Daisy shuffles nervously beside me. Ash gives me a nudge and a goofy wink.

"Second prize goes to Daniel Diaz of Walnut Hills Elementary School."

I feel Carmen-Daisy's clammy hand in mine. She's gripping far too tightly. It's making me *verrrry* nervous.

"And first prize . . . goes to . . ."

Just then, the letter flutters right out of Miss B's shaky hands. I hold my breath. Mr. Popart comes forward and hands it back to Miss B.

"Oh, Andrew," she says, straightening her spectacles, "why don't you read it for us? Go on . . . please!"

Mr. Popart straightens out the paper and begins reading in his lovely voice, "And the first prize goes to . . . our very own . . . Bettina Valentino of Bayside Prep for her painting entitled *The Storm*."

I can't believe it! Maybe I've imagined it! Maybe this is a dream. I mean, these things only happen in stories, right?

But the crowd goes wild. I feel the noise under my feet. It's enough to knock the peeling paint off the walls. Carmen-Daisy lifts me into the air and shakes me like bag of popcorn. Sometimes she gets just a bit too excited. I ask her to put me down.

Mr. Popart has more to read. He raises his hand for quiet.

"The judges say: 'The feeling of stormy weather was masterfully captured in this mixed-media work of art. The symbolism of destruction, as seen in the broken surface, makes a powerful statement about man's battle against the elements of nature.'"

"And Maxine Rattle's foot," Mason whispers.

Then Miss B returns and has something more to say: "As you know, the prize of five hundred dollars goes to the winner. But in addition, I'm delighted to announce that Smooth as Satin Paint Company—renowned for their high-quality finishes—has added an extra wonderful surprise. They have offered to supply enough paint for us to be able to repaint our entire school over the summer! Thank you, dear, dear Bettina! Do come up and receive your prize."

Carmen-Daisy gives me a push forward and I go tottering toward the stage. Mr. Popart is there to take my hand and lead me up the stairs. Another loud round of applause and I feel my knees start to wobble. But he holds my hand all the way to where Miss B's standing. She has an envelope for me.

"Speech, speech!"

I recognize Mason's wild-boy voice. Soon others join in.

"Speech, Speech, Speech!"

Miss B lowers the microphone and steps aside.

"Go on, Bettina, take a deep breath and *enunciate*."

I do take a deep breath, and suddenly I have something to say.

"I'd like to thank Mr. Popart for everything that he's done for us. He's the best art teacher in the world. Before he came to Bayside, I didn't really know what I wanted to be when I grow up. Now I do. I want to be an artist like Picasso . . . and Mr. Popart. Maybe some of you have heard about the Picasso Club that we've started. Well, Mr. Popart's going to help us put on our first art exhibition. So if any of you would like to join, that would be cool, because we want to raise lots of money for the school and Old Boobs—"

Laughter flutters through the hall and I quickly correct myself.

"I mean, to make the school and the statue of Ernestine Bublé, the founder of Bayside, look nice and new."

Miss B gives me a kind, wonky smile and guides me off the stage. As I pass Mr. Popart, he catches my eye and gives me a high five. I float back to my Picasso Club friends on a wave of applause, clutching my prize . . . and trying really hard not to blush.

But when I get back to Carmen-Daisy, she nudges me.

"Bettina Valentino, will you please tell me why you've turned the color of Mr. Popart's pink trousers?"

"Oh, pink shtink!" I say, giving her a bump toward Mason.

"Take it easy, Car!" he says. But I can tell that he really likes having her bump into him.

"Now who's turned pink?" I tease her right back.

"Have not!" she says, fighting off the giggles.

"As pink as a baby's bum," I whisper.

Suddenly she starts shaking like a lump of pink Jell-O being slapped around from all sides. As soon as we're out of the hall, we collapse into a hopeless heap of hysterics. Kids step over us. They must think we've totally lost it!

Giggling is like that, isn't it? You do kind of lose it. Okay, boys may think it's silly. But Car calls it "girl power" because, she says, it's something that girls can do better than anyone else in the whole wide world, PLUS only *we* know what we're giggling about.

Don't know about that.

But I do know that . . .

. . . when I'm lying in a puddle of giggles with my best friend at my side AND I've just won a big prize for one of my paintings, it's simply got to be . . . THE BIGGEST I'LL-NEVER-FORGET-THIS MOMENT OF MY ENTIRE *FAB-U-LOUS* LIFE.

So far!